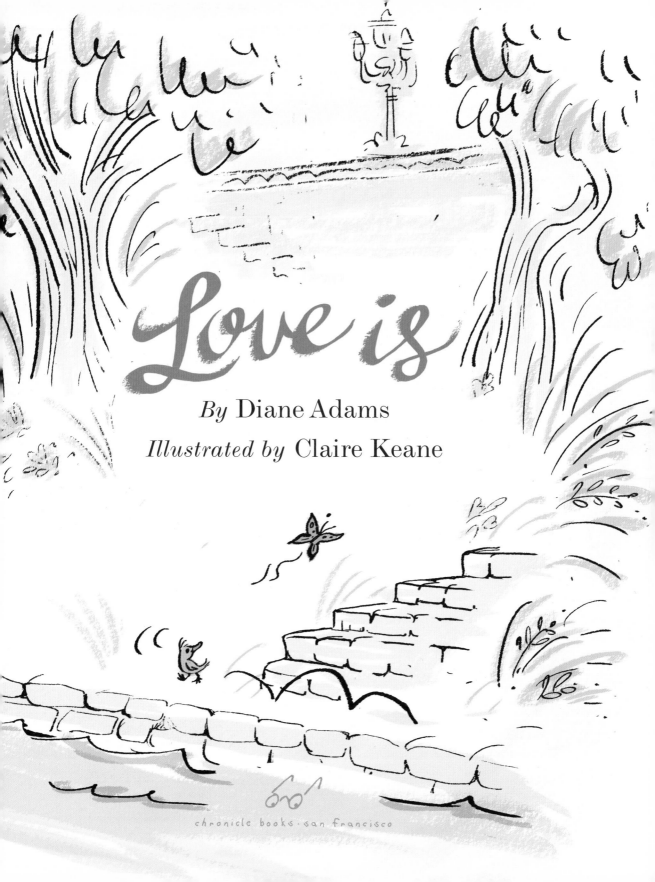

# Love is

By Diane Adams

Illustrated by Claire Keane

chronicle books · san francisco

Love is holding something fragile,
tiny wings and downy head.

Love is noisy midnight feedings,
shoe box right beside the bed.

It's peaceful sleeping, no more peeping,
tucked in tightly, head to toes.

Love is waking up together,
side by side, and beak to nose.

It's early mornings,

messy bath times,

tidying up,

and settling down.

Love is in familiar voices,
feeling lost, and being found.

It's in the struggles,
growing muscles,

ready for a bigger pond.

It's sensing when the time is right
to lift those wings, to travel on.

Love is nudging, gently tugging,
coaxing baby from the nest.

It's getting to the edge and hoping,
letting nature do the rest.

Love is missing,

reminiscing,

wishing things could stay the same.

It's understanding even ducklings,
like the seasons, have to change.

And love is also watching, waving, wondering if love remembers you,

and knowing in a happy instant,
that love has lasted . . .

...and grown some, too.

*For Katy, Kate, and Kelli, three extraordinary*
*sisters-in-law, and my mom-in-law, Jane,*
*who is pretty extraordinary herself!*

*Hugs and endless thanks to Melissa Manlove,*
*Kelly Sonnack, Julie Romeis Sanders, and*
*Andrea Fingerson. It takes a village —D.A.*

*For my lovely mom —C.K.*

Library of Congress Cataloging-in-Publication Data:
Names: Adams, Diane, 1960- author. | Keane, Claire, illustrator.
Title: Love is / by Diane Adams ; illustrated by Claire Keane.
Description: San Francisco : Chronicle Books, [2017] | Summary:
A girl finds a baby duckling, and discovers that love is taking care of
something that needs you, and also knowing when to let it go.
Identifiers: LCCN 2016005490 | ISBN 9781452139975 (alk. paper)
Subjects: LCSH: Ducklings—Juvenile fiction. | Responsibility—
Juvenile fiction. | CYAC: Stories in rhyme. | Ducks—Fiction. |
Animals—Infancy—Fiction. | Love—Fiction. | Responsibility—
Fiction. | Classification: LCC PZ8.3.A100357 Lo 2017 |
DDC 813.6—dc23 LC record available
at http://lccn.loc.gov/2016005490

Manufactured in China.

MIX
Paper from
responsible sources
FSC
www.fsc.org
FSC™ C008047

Design by Amelia Mack.
Typeset in Monotype Modern.
The illustrations in this book were rendered in Photoshop.

10 9 8 7 6 5 4 3 2 1

Chronicle Books LLC
680 Second Street
San Francisco, California 94107
www.chroniclekids.com